Curious George
takes a Job

H. A. REY

SCHOLASTIC INC.
New York Toronto London Auckland Sydney

There are more books about Curious George. You may want to read:

*CURIOUS GEORGE

*CURIOUS GEORGE RIDES A BIKE

*CURIOUS GEORGE GETS A MEDAL

 CURIOUS GEORGE FLIES A KITE

 CURIOUS GEORGE LEARNS THE ALPHABET

*Available from Scholastic

ISBN 0-590-33892-7

36 35 34   3 4 5 6 7/0

This is George. He lived in the Zoo.

He was a good little monkey — but he was very curious.

He wanted to find out what was going on outside the Zoo.

One day, when the keeper was not paying attention,
George got hold of the key for the cage.

When the keeper discovered what had happened, it was too late – George was gone!

WHERE
WAS GEORGE?

They looked for him everywhere.

But they could not find him.

George was hiding in the hay of his friend, the elephant. Finally the keepers gave up looking for him.

George found a nice cozy spot to sleep under the elephant's right ear, and the next morning, before the Zoo opened, he got away safely.

Once in the street, George felt a little scared. What should he do in the big city? Maybe he could find his friend, the man with the yellow hat, who had brought him over from Africa a long time ago. Only George did not know where he lived.

There was a bus stopping at the corner. George had never ridden on one. Quickly he climbed a lamp post, jumped on top of the bus, and off they went.

Now they were right
in the center of the town.
There was so much to see
that George did not know
where to look first.

If only he
could go on riding
like this forever!

But after a while George got tired and a little dizzy.
When the bus slowed down to turn into a side street,
George jumped off.

There was a restaurant right in front of him.
Mmmm — something smelled good! Suddenly George
felt very hungry.

The kitchen door stood open and George walked in.

On the table was a big pot. Of course George was curious. He had to find out what was in it...

When the cook came back, he had a big surprise. Spaghetti was all over the place, and in the middle of it was a little monkey!

George had been eating yards and yards, and had wound himself all up in it.

The cook was a kind man and did not scold much. But George had to clean up the kitchen and then do all the dishes. My, what a lot of them there were! The cook was watching George. "You are lucky to have four hands," he said. "You can do things twice as quickly.

"I have a friend who could use a handy little fellow like you to wash windows. If you would like to, I will take you over to him."

So they went down into the subway and took an uptown train to the cook's friend, who was an elevator man in a skyscraper.

"Sure, I can use you, George!" the elevator man said. "I will give you what you need for the job. You can start right away. But remember — you are here for washing windows. Never mind what people inside the house are doing. Don't be curious, or you'll get into trouble."

George promised to be good, but little monkeys sometimes forget...

George was ready to start. My, how many windows there were! But George got ahead quickly, since he worked with all four hands. He jumped from window to window, just as he had once jumped from tree to tree in the African jungle.

For a while George stuck to his work and did not pay any attention to the people inside. Of course he was curious, but he remembered his promise.

In one room a little boy was crying because he did not want to eat his spinach. George did not even look, but went right on with his work.

In another room a man was taking a nap and snoring. George was sorry it was not his friend, the man with the yellow hat. He listened to the funny noise for a while, then went on working.

But what was going on in here? George stopped working and pressed his nose against the window. Two painters were working inside. George was fascinated. Painting looked like a lot more fun than washing windows!

The painters were getting ready to go out for lunch.
The minute they left, George climbed inside.

What wonderful paints and brushes they had!
George could not resist...

An hour later the painters came back. They opened
the door — and stood there with their mouths wide open.
The whole room had changed into a jungle, with palm
trees all over the walls and a giraffe and two leopards

and a zebra. And a little monkey was busy painting himself on one of the trees!

Then the painters knew what had happened!

Luckily, George was close to a door. He ran out as fast as he could. After him ran the two painters, then the elevator man, and then the woman who lived in the place.

"Oh, my lovely room, my lovely room!" cried the woman. "Don't let him get away!"

George headed for the fire escape.

George reached the end of the fire escape.

The others had not caught up with him yet.

Here was his chance. They could not jump!

But George could easily jump down and escape.

In a moment he would be safe!

Poor little George! He had forgotten that the pavement was hard as stone — not like the soft grass of the jungle.

Too bad! The fall broke his leg, and an ambulance came to take George to the hospital.

"He got what he deserved!" said the woman. "Making my apartment into a jungle, indeed!"

"I told him he would get into trouble," the elevator man added. "He was too curious."

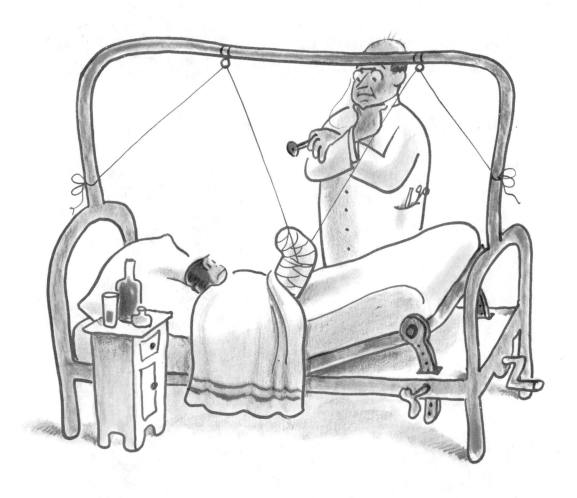

George had to lie in bed with his leg high up in a plaster cast. He was very unhappy.

And it had all started out so nicely! If only he had not been so curious, he could have had a lot of fun. Now it was too late.

But next morning George's friend, the man with the
big yellow hat, was buying his newspaper. Suddenly he
got very excited. "This is George!" he shouted when he

saw the picture on the front page. Quickly he read the whole story, and then ran to a telephone booth to ring the hospital.

"I am George's friend," he said to the nurse who answered the telephone. "Please take good care of him so that he will get better quickly. I want to take him to a movie studio and make a picture about his life in the jungle. Don't let him get into any more mischief until I can take him away."

Finally the day came when George could walk again.

"Your friend is going to take you away this morning," said the nurse. "Just wait right here for him, and don't touch anything!"

As soon as George was alone, he looked around at all the strange hospital things. "I wonder what is in that big bottle," he thought.

George was very curious.

It smelled funny!

Suddenly his head began to turn.

Then he felt as if he were flying.

Then rings and stars danced before his eyes,

then everything went dark...

And this is how the man with
the yellow hat found George when he came to call for
him! They picked him up and shook him, but they could
not wake him up.

He was so fast asleep that finally they had to put him

UNDER THE SHOWER!

How surprised he was when he woke up!

George said good-by to the nurse and the kind doctor. Then he and the man with the yellow hat got into the car to drive to the movie studio.

MOVI
STUDI

In the president's office, George had to sign a contract. Now he was a movie actor!

In the studio, George was kept so busy all the time that he forgot to be curious. He liked the jungle they made for him, and played happily there.

And when the picture was finally finished, George invited all his friends to see it: the doctor and the nurse and the ambulance driver and the man from the newsstand and the woman and the elevator man and the two painters and the cook and the reporter and all the keepers of the Zoo.

Now the lights went out and the picture started.

"This is George," the voice began.

"He lived in the jungle.

He was a good little monkey —

he had only one fault: he was too curious."